W9-AYD-810

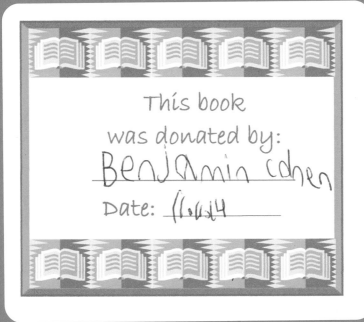

This book
was donated by:
BenjAmin cohen
Date: 11.4.14

LIKE CARROT JUICE

ON A CUPCAKE

DISCARD

Franklin School
Summit Public Schools

LIKE CARROT JUICE ON A CUPCAKE

BY JULIE STERNBERG

ILLUSTRATIONS BY MATTHEW CORDELL

Amulet Books, New York

PUBLISHER'S NOTE: This is a work of fiction. Names, characters, places, and incidents are either the product of the author's imagination or are used fictitiously, and any resemblance to actual persons, living or dead, business establishments, events, or locales is entirely coincidental.

Library of Congress Cataloging-in-Publication Data
Sternberg, Julie.
Like carrot juice on a cupcake / by Julie Sternberg ; illustrations by Matthew Cordell.
pages cm
Sequel to: Like bug juice on a burger.
Summary: "A new girl at school throws nine-year-old Eleanor's relationship with her best friend Pearl into disarray" — Provided by publisher.
ISBN 978-1-4197-1033-9
[1. Novels in verse. 2. Best friends—Fiction. 3. Friendship—Fiction. 4. Schools—Fiction.]
I. Cordell, Matthew, 1975– illustrator. II. Title.
PZ7.5.S74Lg 2014
[Fic]—dc23
2013023276

Text copyright © 2014 Julie Sternberg
Illustrations copyright © 2014 Matthew Cordell
Book design by Jessie Gang

Published in 2014 by Amulet Books, an imprint of ABRAMS. All rights reserved. No portion of this book may be reproduced, stored in a retrieval system, or transmitted in any form or by any means, mechanical, electronic, photocopying, recording, or otherwise, without written permission from the publisher. Amulet Books and Amulet Paperbacks are registered trademarks of Harry N. Abrams, Inc.

Printed and bound in U.S.A.
10 9 8 7 6 5 4 3 2 1

Amulet Books are available at special discounts when purchased in quantity for premiums and promotions as well as fundraising or educational use. Special editions can also be created to specification. For details, contact specialsales@abramsbooks.com or the address below.

ABRAMS
THE ART OF BOOKS SINCE 1949

115 West 18th Street
New York, NY 10011
www.abramsbooks.com

FOR MY PAUL

—J. S.

I did a mean thing.

A very mean thing.

To a new girl AND

to my best friend.

I HATE that I did it.

But I did.

This is worse than

carrot juice on a cupcake

or a wasp on my pillow

or a dress that's too tight at the neck.

I hope you never do anything that mean.

I really do.

CHAPTER ONE

It all started one Monday morning in April
when our fourth-grade teacher,
Mrs. Ramji,
made a special announcement.
She was standing near her desk,
beside a girl I'd never seen before.
That girl wore sparkly clothes
and a headband with a big bow.
"We have a new student!" Mrs. Ramji said.
"This is Ainsley Biggs.
She just moved here, from Orlando!"
"*Orlando!*" my best friend, Pearl, whispered to me,
from the desk beside mine.
"How *magical.*"
I heard other kids whisper, "Disney!"

And then the boy who sits behind me,

Nicholas Rigby,

started humming the Disney song

"It's a Small World."

He hummed and hummed,

just loud enough for me to hear.

"Shh!" I told him.

I turned and glared at him, too.

Because Nicholas Rigby is always

getting us in trouble.

Plus, I knew I'd never get that song out of my head.

"Doesn't Ainsley look like a present?"

Pearl whispered to me.

"A shiny present, too pretty to unwrap?"

(Pearl talks like a poet sometimes.)

"She *does* look like a present!" I whispered back.

I started wondering

whether *I* ever wanted to look like a present.

2

Before I could decide,

Mrs. Ramji turned the lights off

and on again

to get our attention.

"Class 4A!" she said.

"Please settle down!

You're not behaving your best for Ainsley.

We need to make her feel welcome!

It's not easy,

starting a new school so late in the year."

Then Mrs. Ramji said,

"Pearl!"

Pearl sat up straighter,

and I did, too.

Because maybe she was in trouble.

But Mrs. Ramji told Pearl,

"I would like you to move your desk

closer to Eleanor's, please."

"*Closer* to Eleanor's?" Pearl asked.

3

"Yes," Mrs. Ramji said.
"Actually, everyone in that row,
move a little
to make space for Ainsley's desk,
on the other side of Pearl."
"Yay! Closer to you!"
Pearl whispered to me,
and we grinned at each other
as everyone in our row
started making space for Ainsley.
After we'd finished
and I'd sat back down,
a wadded-up ball of paper flew
through the air
and landed on my desk.
I knew exactly
what that flying paper was.
I opened it up
and smoothed it out.

Sure enough, Nicholas Rigby had drawn me a picture.

This one showed me on a roller coaster

in Orlando,

with my arms in the air

and my hair blowing in crazy directions.

I folded the picture neatly

and put it on top of the pile

of Nicholas's pictures

that I kept in my desk.

Because even though that boy's impossible,

he's still a ridiculously good drawer.

Then I turned and whispered to him,

"Thanks."

Like I always did.

And he kicked the back of my chair,

not too hard,

like *he* always did.

Then Mrs. Ramji asked us

to take out our Creative Writing notebooks

and work on our Brooklyn Bridge poems

while she and Pearl helped Ainsley get set up.

I loved my Brooklyn Bridge poem.

So I worked on it very hard.

And realized only later

that I should've been

paying attention to Ainsley instead.

Because during that time,

she started casting a glittery spell over Pearl.

She really did.

CHAPTER TWO

Pearl came home from school with me that afternoon.

Because it was a Monday.

And Pearl always came home from school with me

on Mondays.

Wednesdays, too.

(Because her mom was still at work.)

We loved those afternoons.

We usually trained my little dog, Antoine.

And did our homework.

And baked, when we had time.

That Monday

we had time.

So we decided to make chocolate cupcakes.

My very nice babysitter, Natalie,

preheated the oven,

then left the room for a minute.

Antoine sat right behind us,

ready to lick or chew anything that fell.

"We can't drop *any* chocolate," I reminded Pearl.

"It's poisonous for dogs."

"Right!" Pearl said.

She pushed the cocoa to the back of the counter.

Then we took turns measuring ingredients

and dumping them in a bowl

and mixing them together.

We had no problems at all.

Until

it was time

for the salt.

I should've measured the salt over the sink.

But we'd done everything else so perfectly!

I figured I could do the salt perfectly, too!

So, with my right hand,

I held a teaspoon over our bowl.

And with my left hand,

I tilted a big salt container,

with a fast-pouring spout,

over that little teaspoon.

One second later,

a *mountain* of salt appeared

on top of our beautiful batter.

"Aaagghhh!" I cried,

watching as that mountain started sinking.

"Oh no, oh no!" Pearl cried.

Natalie rushed in. "What happened?" she said.

Then Antoine ran over to Natalie,

but Natalie didn't see him,

so Natalie tripped on Antoine,

and Antoine yelped a terrible yelp.

Both Pearl and I cried, "Antoine!"

and turned to comfort him.

But as I turned,

I hit the wooden spoon we'd been using in our batter.

Our *chocolate* batter.

And the chocolate-covered spoon flew
out of the bowl and onto the floor.

Antoine must not have been hurt at all.

Because he *zoomed* to that spoon
and started licking up the chocolate!

"No, Antoine!" I cried. "It's poison!"

Natalie grabbed one end of the spoon,
but Antoine held on to the other
and they ended up playing tug-of-war.

"Drop it, Antoine!" I cried. "Drop it!"

But he didn't listen.

Then Pearl,

who is a dog-training genius,

grabbed a bag of Antoine's treats

and held it open,

right under his nose.

"Come, Antoine!" she said, backing up. "Come!"

Like a miracle,

Antoine dropped the spoon

and went to Pearl.

She fed him lots of treats,

and we both hugged him

while Natalie called the vet.

"He's going to be fine," she told us,

after she'd hung up.

"He might throw up a little later,

but that'd just be a sign

that he's getting bad things out of his system."

After that happy news,

Pearl and I turned back to our cupcakes.

We tried to take out the thin layer of salt
still resting at the top of the batter.
Then we finished everything else.
We'd just gotten the cupcakes in the oven
when my dad came home.
He was whistling "Hey Jude," by the Beatles.
(My dad *loves* the Beatles.)
And
as soon as he saw me and Pearl washing dishes,
he started making up a song to that tune.
He sang:
"He-ey *Pearl*, in my kit-*chen*.
Baking sweet *things*
with my El-ea-*nor*."
I stopped him then.
Because he was being ridiculous!
Also, he does *not* sing well.
Pearl laughed, though.
And my dad gave us both hugs.

A little later,
when Pearl's mom came to pick Pearl up,
my dad said,
"You can't have her! She's *ours.*"
He liked saying that, every Monday and Wednesday.
I liked hearing it, too.
Because I loved thinking of Pearl as ours.

CHAPTER THREE

The next morning,
I brought most of the cupcakes to school
on a plastic plate, all covered in foil.
For Pearl.
"They're pretty salty," I told her,
handing her the plate.
"But they're not terrible."
We were standing at our desks,
waiting for the first bell to ring.
"Thanks," she said.
Then she asked, "How's Antoine?
Did he throw up?"
"Yes!" I told her. "Right before I went to bed!
All over my mom's favorite rug!
She was *not* happy."

"But vomiting was good for him!" Pearl said.

"He was getting bad things out of his system."

"I *told* my mom that," I said.

"She said, 'I'm very glad they're out of his system.
But do they have to be on my rug?'"

Somebody behind us started making

yucky vomiting noises then.

I didn't even turn around.

I knew who it was.

"Stop listening to our conversations, Nicholas!"

I said.

"And stop being disgusting!"

"I'm getting bad things out of my system," he said.

At that moment, the new girl, Ainsley, walked in.
She looked very sparkly and colorful,
just like the day before.
And she had on another big bow.
"Hey, Ainsley!" Pearl and I both said
as Ainsley walked to her desk.
"Hey," she said back.
She seemed a little shy.
"Want a cupcake?" Pearl asked her,
holding up the foil-covered plate.

"They're salty!" Nicholas called out from behind us.
"*Stop* listening to our *conversations*!"
I told Nicholas again.
"They *are* a little salty," Pearl told Ainsley.
"It's okay," Ainsley said. "I'm not really hungry.
Thanks, though."
I don't know what Pearl said next,
because Nicholas distracted me
by throwing a wadded-up piece of paper at my arm.

"Ow!" I said, when it hit me,
even though it didn't hurt at all.
Then I picked that ball of paper up off the floor
and smoothed it out.
It was a picture of me,
with chocolate all over my face,
eating a giant cupcake.

I folded that picture
and put it on top of my Nicholas picture pile
and thanked him,
the way I always did.
Then I heard Ainsley say to Pearl,
"They're so good, they're *crazy*.
You should come bake them at my house with me!"
I frowned a little.
I didn't love
Ainsley inviting Pearl to her house
to bake *crazy*-delicious things.
But

the very next moment,

Ainsley turned to me and said,

super-nicely,

"You should come, too!

We'll all make them together."

"Make what?" I asked.

"Brookie cupcakes!" she said.

"They're brownies and chocolate chip cookies

mixed together,

inside cupcakes."

My mouth fell open.

I had to admit,

I had never *dreamed* of anything as good

as brownies *and* chocolate chip cookies

inside cupcakes.

"Is there frosting?" I asked Ainsley.

"Chocolate frosting," she said.

"We'll definitely make them with you,"

Pearl told Ainsley.

"Right, Eleanor?"

"Of course!" I said.

I really meant that, too.

And not just because I wanted to taste those things.

I thought Natalie would take me and Pearl

over to Ainsley's

on a Monday or a Wednesday.

And we'd all have fun together.

Then,

Pearl and I—

best friends for our whole lives—

would go back to our Mondays and Wednesdays

together.

Just the two of us.

I was *sure* that was how it would happen.

But

it turned out, I had no idea

about anything.

CHAPTER FOUR

Everything started changing that night after dinner,

when Pearl called me up on the phone.

"Eleanor!" she shouted. "It's Pearl!"

"Pearl!" I shouted back.

(That's how we like to start our calls.)

"I have news," she said. "It's exciting news

and miserable news, too.

All blended up."

"What are you talking about?" I said.

"I get to be Ainsley's buddy!" she said.

I was quiet for a second.

Every new kid at our school is assigned a buddy,

to help with schoolwork and making friends.

And for that one second, I couldn't help wondering,

Why hadn't Mrs. Ramji picked *me*

to be Ainsley's buddy?

Wouldn't *I* be a good one?

Then I told myself,

Stop being stupid.

And I said to Pearl, "That's great!

Why isn't it only exciting?"

"Because of this miserable part," Pearl said.

"Ainsley is far behind.

So her buddy needs to help her with homework

every Monday and Wednesday, after school.

Until she catches up."

"*Monday* and *Wednesday*?" I said.

"Yes," she said. Her voice was sad.

"No other days work."

"But no other days work for us, either," I said,

thinking of Pearl's Hebrew school, and my art classes,

and Pearl's weekend house upstate.

"I know," she said.

We were both quiet for a second.

Then I asked, "When does the homework help start?"
I hoped she'd at least say, "Monday,"
so we'd have the next afternoon,
a Wednesday,
together.
Instead, she said, quietly, "Tomorrow."
"For how many weeks?" I asked.
"I don't know," she said.
"I don't know when she'll get caught up."
"I hope she's very smart," I said.
I stood silently then,
holding the phone and wondering
how much time they'd spend studying together
and baking brookies together
and eating those crazy-delicious things together
while I was at home alone,
missing Pearl.
And then I almost dropped the phone!
Because I saw Antoine

hurrying happily by

with one of my mom's fancy scarves

in his mouth.

"Antoine! Scarf!" I told Pearl.

She knew exactly what I meant.

"Hurry, hurry, hurry!" she said.

We hung up,

then I hurried

and found Antoine by the couch in our living room,

pulling and chewing on the scarf.

"No, Antoine, no!" I cried.

I got the scarf away from him,

but already

it was very slobbery.

And very ripped.

I knew that rip meant big trouble.

Just the week before,

Antoine had eaten one of my dad's dressy shoes

and left bite marks

on one leg of our coffee table.

And, of course, he'd just vomited on my mom's rug.

(Which was *not* his fault.)

I lay on my stomach then

and looked right into Antoine's eyes.

"*I* forgive you," I said.

"But Mom and Dad are going to be *mad*."

Antoine licked my nose very sweetly.

"At least scarves aren't poisonous," I told him,

scratching behind his ears.

Then I shoved Mom's scarf deep inside my pocket.

I meant to hide it in her scarf drawer

sometime before bed.

But I got distracted

by homework and bath time and sadness about Pearl.

And,

very

stupidly,

I forgot all about that scarf.

CHAPTER FIVE

When I got to school the next morning,
Pearl and Ainsley were already in the music room,
waiting for class to start.
I stopped near the door to the room for a second,
watching them laugh together.
Pearl kept smiling
even after they'd stopped laughing.
And I could see
that she might be very, very happy
on Mondays and Wednesdays,
with Ainsley.
And without me.

The morning bell rang then,
and everyone started sitting on the music room rug.

I walked toward my usual spot,

where I'd sat every other day for the entire year.

But before I could get there,

Ainsley took it!

My spot!

Right between Pearl and our friend Katie.

Pearl didn't try to stop Ainsley.

But she didn't forget me, either.

She scooted over and made a space for me

between her and red-haired, freckly Ben.

I didn't want to sit next to Ben,

who can be mean sometimes.

But I couldn't exactly fight with the new girl

over a space on the rug.

So I sat.

And Pearl said,

"Listen to this joke Ainsley told me earlier!"

I leaned closer to her, to listen.

"Why should you close your eyes

when you open the fridge?" Pearl said.

"I don't know," I said.

"So you don't see the salad dressing!" Pearl said.

"Isn't that *hilarious*?"

Normally I would've laughed.

But I wasn't in a laughing mood.

So I only smiled a little.

Pearl noticed.

"You're sad," she said,

losing all her laughter.

Then she said, "I bet I know why.

I've been worrying about this.

You don't want to be alone

on Mondays and Wednesdays. Right?"

I nodded.

We both knew that I wouldn't actually be alone.

I'd be with Natalie and Antoine.

But still.

I'd be missing my best friend.

Pearl frowned.

Then our music teacher, Mrs. Quaid,

clapped her hands to get our attention.

"Time to begin," she said.

"And what a day we're going to have!

As most of you know,

every year I write a springtime musical

about bunnies

for the fourth graders,

who perform it in front of the whole lower school

and fourth-grade parents.

Who remembers last year's hit,

Mary Hoppins?"

Lots of kids raised their hands, including me.

I'd liked that show, about a magical bunny nanny.

"This year," Mrs. Quaid said,

"we'll put on

A Tale of Two Bunnies.

It's very loosely based on a book for adults—

A Tale of Two Cities, by Charles Dickens.

Raise your hand if you've heard of it."

Only nice Adam,

whose hair always sticks up a little in the back,
raised his hand.
"My mom loves that book," he said.
"As well she should," Mrs. Quaid said.
"And I know you'll all love the musical, too.
Now, our show must be cast!
To play a role,
you must be free for rehearsals Mondays,
Wednesdays, and Fridays.
Who will be the first to audition?"
Pearl leaned close to me then
and whispered,
"I have the most brilliant idea!"
Before I could say a word,
she was waving her arm in the air and yelling,
"Eleanor! Eleanor wants to audition!"
"*What?*" I cried.
I did *not* want to audition.
I did *not* want to sing in front of the class

or the whole lower school
and fourth-grade parents!
I started pulling down
on Pearl's arm.
But she kept her arm up.
I had no idea she was so strong!
"You need something to do in the afternoons!"
she told me, in a very bossy whisper.
"Or you'll be sad and lonely!"
"I don't like singing in front of people!"
I whispered back. "You *know* that!"
"What's happening over there?" Mrs. Quaid asked.
"Would you like to audition, Eleanor?"
"Yes!" Pearl said,
before I could open my mouth.
"She's just scared of singing in front of people,"
Pearl said.
I glared at her.
I didn't want her *announcing* that!

"Sorry!" she whispered. "But I'm doing it for *you*!"

"Ah," Mrs. Quaid said.

"Stage fright.

It's important to nip that in the bud.

It can become quite debilitating.

I have an idea.

Pearl, why don't you audition *with* Eleanor?"

"I wish I could," Pearl said,

sounding miserable. "But I can't come to rehearsals

on Mondays and Wednesdays."

"I'll do it!" someone shouted from across the room.

I recognized that voice.

Sure enough, Nicholas Rigby

popped up from his place on the floor.

"You *will*?" I said,

shocked.

And Mrs. Quaid looked as surprised

as if she'd just seen a flying trumpet.

Because Nicholas had never done *anything* in music

except get in trouble

for burping to the tune of "God Bless America."

(He's a ridiculously good burper.)

"I'm ready," Nicholas said,

walking over to Mrs. Quaid.

Then he asked me, "Are you ready?"

I still hesitated.

Pearl elbowed me.

And Mrs. Quaid said,

"Let's conquer that stage fright, Eleanor."

So I went to stand beside Nicholas.

"This is marvelous!" Mrs. Quaid said.

"What song will you two sing?"

"I've got one," Nicholas said.

Then he sang, "You better watch out,"

and paused

and looked at me.

And waited

and waited

for me to sing the next line.

What else could I do?

"You better not cry," I sang. Quietly.

"Yay, Eleanor!" Pearl shouted.

Other kids started laughing.

Maybe because we weren't the greatest singers.

Or maybe because we were singing a Christmas song

in *April*.

Nicholas ignored them and kept singing.

So I did, too.

I got a little louder by the end.

And

after the last "Santa Claus is coming to town,"

everyone cheered.

"That was very brave, Eleanor," Mrs. Quaid said.

"And very kind, Nicholas.

Now, who's next?"

Nicholas and I sat back down.

Si-ilent ni-ight

Pearl hugged me

as nice Adam stood up and started singing

"Silent Night,"

very beautifully.

Then freckly Ben sang "Frosty the Snowman."

And tall Nora, with her brand-new glasses,

sang "Jingle Bells."

And short Kai sang

"Rudolph the Red-Nosed Reindeer."

Frosty, the Snowman

When Kai finished, Mrs. Quaid sang out,

to the tune of "White Christmas,"

"I'm dreaming of a

different song theme."

But kids kept singing Christmas tunes.

Our friend Katie started "The Little Drummer Boy."

"You know what's *tragic*?"

Pearl whispered to me

during Katie's *pa-rum-pa-pum-pums*.

"What?" I whispered back.

"It's tragic that Ainsley can't be in the show,"

Pearl whispered.

"Since she can't go to rehearsals, either.

Did you know she was Beauty

in her third grade's performance of

Beauty and the Beast?"

I shook my head.

I wondered how Pearl knew.

I wondered if I'd ever be a Beauty.

Then I peeked around Pearl, to glance at Ainsley.

And I wondered if she was ever going to take off

that humongous bow.

CHAPTER SIX

I thought I'd have a happy dinner that night
with my parents.
I thought I'd tell them about the audition right away.
And they'd be so proud of me,
for overcoming my fears.
But it wasn't a happy dinner at all.
When I walked into the kitchen,
they were both already sitting at their places.
They looked up at me.
But neither one of them smiled.

"What's wrong?" I asked, sitting at my place.

There was a big bowl of spaghetti and meatballs
on the table,
but they hadn't served any onto our plates.

"It's Antoine," my dad said.

"Oh no!" I said. "Is he sick?"

Antoine had followed me into the kitchen.

As I looked down at him,

he put his paws up on my chair

and started wagging his whole body.

I touched his nose, to see if it was dry,

and he licked my hand.

He *seemed* fine.

But maybe I was missing something.

"Did he throw up again?" I asked.

"He's healthy," my mom said.

Then she pointed,

and I realized.

Her ripped-up scarf was lying near her plate.

"Oh," I said,

and sank a little in my seat.

"I found it in your pocket," my dad said.

"This morning, after you'd gone to school.

When I picked your clothes up off the floor

to put them in the hamper."

I sank even lower.

Why didn't I *ever* remember

to put my clothes in the hamper myself?

"I should've kept that scarf safe in a drawer,"

my mom said. "That was my mistake.

Still, we shouldn't have to worry all the time.

Antoine needs to be trained."

That got me mad!

"I *am* training him!" I said.

Hadn't they been paying attention?

Pearl and I had been working so hard!

"Watch," I said.

I pushed my chair back

and stood up tall over Antoine
and pointed at the ground
and said, loudly,
"Sit!"

Sit!

He didn't sit.

Woof!

Instead, he wagged his tail a little
and barked back at me.

I felt mad at Pearl then.
She could *always* get him to sit.
Why couldn't she be here now,
when I needed her?
She was probably on the phone with stupid Ainsley,
listening to *hilarious* jokes.

"Sit, Antoine!" I said again,
trying not to think about Pearl.

"Sit!

Sit!"

Finally, he sat.

"Good dog!" I said,

and gave him a hug.

"See?" I told my parents.

"He can lie down, too. And shake.

You *know* that."

"We *do* know that," my mom said.

"You've been working hard," my dad said.

"But you need help," my mom said.

"The chewing has been a problem for a while.

And as you told me, you tried to get him

to drop that chocolate-covered spoon,

but he didn't listen. That's not safe for *him*."

I shouldn't have told you! I thought.

"Also," my mom continued, "he nips sometimes.

And jumps quite a lot."

"He's only playing when he nips," I said.

My mom ignored that.

"I've done some research," she said.

"There's a doggie training camp in the country

that gets rave reviews.

It's only two weeks,

and I think it'll do a world of good."

"Two weeks!" I said.

My sleepaway camp the summer before

had lasted almost two weeks.

So I knew:

Two weeks can take *forever*.

"Starting Sunday," my mom said.

"We made the arrangements

after Antoine ate the coffee table."

"You *can't* send him away," I said.

"The time will fly," my mom said.

"And we'll spend hours with a trainer at the end.

The camp's staff will give him a strong foundation,

and teach us how to build on that foundation."

I couldn't believe it.

I'd already lost my favorite times with Pearl.

She'd started tutoring Ainsley that very afternoon.

Now I was losing Antoine, too.

"I'm going with him," I told my parents.

"It's for dogs only," my mom said.

"I'll hide behind Antoine," I said, "and sneak in."

"If only you were smaller than Antoine,"

my mom said.

"And if only you liked dog food," my dad said.

"Because that's all they serve at dog camp."

I remembered then

hating the yucky food at my own camp.

And I knew my dad had a point.

Because I could tell,

just by the smell of Antoine's meals:

Dog food

is even worse

than pickles.

CHAPTER SEVEN

Pearl met me in the school lobby the next morning.
As soon as she saw me,
she started jumping up and down.
"You're a star!" she cried. "A shining star!"
"What are you talking about?" I said.
She took my hand and pulled me down the hall,
all the way to the bulletin board
outside the music room.
Mrs. Quaid had posted the cast list.
"Mama Rabbit: Eleanor Kane,"
the list said.
And,
"Bunny Son: Nicholas Rigby."
Lots of other kids got parts, too.
Katie and Nora and Adam

were cousin cottontails,

which made me happy.

Because I could spend those afternoons with them.

But I was a little worried about my part.

"You don't think I have a solo, do you?"

I asked Pearl.

"You might!" she said, very excited.

"Your part is the first one listed!

It must be big!"

"I don't want a solo!" I said.

Because singing a Christmas song quietly in music class

with someone else

was *not* the same

as singing all by myself

on the school stage

in front of an enormous crowd.

As the day went on,

I hated my role more and more.

Because every time Nicholas walked by my desk,
he said,
"Hey there, Mama!"
And
when Ainsley sat down for lunch with me and Pearl,
she said, "How's your little baby?"
So everyone at the table laughed at me.
Including Pearl!
And *then*,
in the middle of history,
Nicholas passed me a note.
He'd drawn a picture of me
wearing an apron and saying,
"Would you like a fresh carrot, dear?"
That was the first picture of Nicholas's
that I ever ripped up.

After all that,
I thought my day *had* to get better.

But then
Mrs. Quaid handed out
the script.

CHAPTER EIGHT

"I think you're going to *love* this,"
Mrs. Quaid kept saying
as she gave the script to each cast member
at the very end of school.
So I thought I'd love it!
As soon as I got home,
I lay on my bed
and read it all the way through.
And
I did *not*
love it.
It got worse and worse
with every page!

As soon as I'd finished,

I ran to the living room
and shook that script at my parents.

I'd already told them about being cast.

Now I told them,
"I can't be Mama Rabbit!"
"Of *course* you can," my mom said.
"You *were* born to be a star," my dad said.
Then he asked to see the script.
I handed it to him and said,
"Look at page nine!"
He opened to the first page instead.
"You have the very first lines!" he said.
Then he laughed and read them aloud:

"'It was the best of carrots,
it was the worst of carrots.'"

My mom laughed, too.

"Why is that funny?" I asked.

"It's a spoof

of *A Tale of Two Cities*," my mom said.

"Do you know those opening lines?

'It was the best of times,

it was the worst of times.'"

"Of course I don't know them!" I said.

"I'm in fourth grade!"

"See how great it is to be in a show?" my dad said.

"You're learning already!"

"You were supposed to turn to page nine!" I said.

He turned to page nine, and I pointed

at the horrible solo Mama Rabbit sings.

All alone, onstage.

In front of the whole audience.

My parents *knew* how I felt

about singing in front of people.

But they still *grinned* when they saw that solo.

"We're so proud of you," they said,
for the millionth time that afternoon.
And then my dad said,
"It's to the tune of 'Oh My Darling, Clementine'!
Don't you love that song?"
"Not really," I said.
But my parents paid me no attention.
They each held up one side of the script,
and then they sang one verse of my solo together.

They sang:

"'Oh my darling, oh my darling,
oh my darling, Bunny mine.
I am lost without you by me.
How I miss you, Bunny mine.'"

They grinned and clapped for themselves
when they'd finished.
I glared at them.
"What a sweet solo," my mom said.
"You're not even *trying* to understand!"
I said.
"I don't want *any* solo.
And I *definitely* don't want a sweet one!"
"You'd rather have a *mean* solo?" my dad said.
"Yes!" I said. "Look at the words!
Mama Rabbit is separated from her son,
so her heart is broken.
The whole play,
she *longs* for her bunny!
I have to *long* for Nicholas Rigby!
And at the end of the play,
I have to *hug* him!
I am *not* doing that!"

"Nicholas Rigby," my mom said.

"He's the really good artist, right?"

I shrugged.

I didn't feel like saying anything nice about Nicholas.

And then the phone rang.

I stomped away from my frustrating parents

and picked it up.

A voice I loved said,

"Hello?"

"Pearl!" I shouted,

so glad she'd called.

She'd understand why I had to quit the play!

Even if she'd gotten me into it in the first place.

I wanted to tell her *everything*.

Plus,

I was hoping she'd say

that she shouldn't have laughed

when Ainsley asked about my baby.

Instead,
she said,
"Eleanor?"

And I said,
"Yes, of course! It's me.
Did you think it was my mom?"

She laughed a little and said,
"Oops!
I meant to call Ainsley!
I forgot to tell her something!
I'll talk to you tomorrow, okay?
Mom said I could only make one call before bed."

And then she hung up.

I stared at the dead phone.

Why wasn't Pearl calling *me*
with her one call?
Why was she practically hanging up on me,
lightning-fast,
instead?

My dad walked by then,
whistling my solo.
"*This* is the worst of times,"
I told him.

Then, still fully clothed,
I got in bed
and pulled my covers over my head
and tried to force myself
to sleep.

CHAPTER NINE

By the next morning, I'd decided for certain.
I'd quit the play that day.

My parents kept trying to talk me out of it.
"It's such an honor to be cast," my dad said.
And my mom said, "You'll have
a *wonderful* experience.
I'm certain of it."
But I said, "It's *my* decision, right?"
And they both said, "Yes."
So I threw my clothes on.
And they dropped me off at school early.

I wished they'd called Mrs. Quaid
to quit for me.

She won't care, I kept saying to myself
as I walked down the hall to the music room.
I slowly passed bulletin boards
and cubbies
and trophy cases.
Until,
finally,
I reached the music room door.
I took a deep breath
and knocked.

"Come in," Mrs. Quaid called.

She was sitting behind her desk, reading,
when I walked in.
She looked at me,
then held up her book for me to see.
"*A Tale of Two Cities*!" she said.
"I was just considering tweaks to our show.

Did you know the book ends with a beheading?"
"What's a beheading?" I asked.
"When someone's head gets chopped off," she said.
"Very dramatic and moving.
But I don't think Principal Nill would want us
chopping off heads.
Do you agree?"

I did agree.
But I wished I didn't.
Because rolling heads were definitely better
than longing for Nicholas Rigby.

"I'm so glad you came in," Mrs. Quaid said.
"I wanted to tell you something.
Our Mama Rabbit was originally a papa.
But you surprised me, Eleanor!
You have a *terrific* tone to your voice.
I don't know how I missed it before.

I'd like to help you develop it
and show it off."
"Uh . . . ," I said. "Thanks."

I was glad she liked my tone.
But
I wondered,
did we have to develop it in the *play*?
Couldn't we develop it in class?

Before I could ask that, Mrs. Quaid said,

"There's one other thing I'm happy about.

The Mama Rabbit role requires maturity.

I know there's lovey-dovey language in the play.

Not every fourth grader could handle that.

But I'm sure you can."

"You are?" I said.

She nodded and said, "I am."

Then she gave me a big smile.

"I've been going on and on," she said.

"I almost forgot to ask—

why'd you stop by?"

"Uh . . . ," I said again,

trying to think.

I couldn't exactly tell her

that I *wasn't* mature enough

for lovey-dovey language.

I picked another problem.

"I don't want to sing all alone onstage," I said.

Mrs. Quaid beamed at me.

"Of course you don't!" she said.

"You're just like me,

when I was your age,

and so many other kids I've helped.

Don't you worry.

I'm a stage fright pro."

She waved that problem away with her hand.

And then the warning bell rang.

"Off to class you go!" Mrs. Quaid said.

"And *no more worrying!*"

So off to class I went.

But I didn't stop worrying.

Because I could tell—

there would be no quitting now.

I was stuck in the show.

B-B-R-R-I-N-G!!!

CHAPTER TEN

"Where have you *been*?" Pearl whispered to me,

when I hurried into class.

"Tell you later," I whispered back.

Because Mrs. Ramji was already talking.

"Time for science, everyone," she said.

"Today, we're making bouncy balls!

Please divide into groups of three."

I raised my eyebrows at Pearl,

who smiled and nodded.

Then,

before I could say a word,

Pearl smiled and nodded at Ainsley, too.

So Ainsley was in our group.

I wished Pearl had checked with me first.

But Ainsley looked so happy

walking over to us.

I couldn't really get mad.

"All groups, find a lab station," Mrs. Ramji said.

"You'll see a powder there

and a liquid

and a sheet of directions."

At our lab station,

we had a box of powder

and a jar of liquid,

but no sheet of directions.

Because

right before we sat down,

Nicholas Rigby reached over and grabbed our sheet.

"That's ours!" Pearl cried.

She tried to grab it back, but she couldn't.

Because Nicholas was holding it very high

and folding it very tight.

"You're going to get us in trouble!" I told him.

He ignored me

and pulled a pair of scissors from his jeans pocket.

"Don't cut it!" Pearl said.

"Why does he have scissors in his pocket?"
Ainsley said.

"He likes art," I told her.

Nicholas cut and cut,

still holding the sheet high in the air,

then unfolded a people chain

of girls in dresses.

He handed it to me.

It was pretty impressive,

so I had to stop being annoyed at him.

But Pearl didn't stop.

"We can't read our directions!" she said.

"They might as well be in *braille*!

I'm going to tell Mrs. Ramji."

She marched off.

"Uh-oh," Nicholas said.

Then he got very busy,

pretending to work on his lab.

Ainsley and I waited together

for Pearl to get back.

We were both quiet for a while.

I couldn't think of anything to say.

And then Ainsley said to me,

"I heard your parents are sending your dog away."

"You did?" I said.

She nodded.

"Pearl told me," she said.

"They're not 'sending him away,'" I said.

"That sounds like he's going forever.

It's only for two weeks."

She looked serious and said,

"Pearl said you're having trouble training him."

"She *did*?" I said.

Ainsley nodded again.

But that didn't make sense.

Pearl and I had been training Antoine together.

So Pearl knew—

we were doing so well!

"We're not having *trouble*," I told Ainsley.

"It's just that he's a puppy.

He has a lot to learn."

"I know," Ainsley said.

"I had to train our dog,

Jo Jo,

when she was a puppy.

At first I was too nice to her.

I had to get very strict

before she really learned.

Maybe you're too nice to your puppy?

Pearl said you probably are."

"*Pearl* said that?" I said.

I was starting to imagine

Pearl and Ainsley with their heads together,

talking and talking,

all about *me*.

"What else has Pearl said?" I asked Ainsley.

"Nothing," she said.

But before I could even start feeling relieved,

Ainsley said,

"Pearl's really happy you're in the musical.

She says you sing like a heavenly angel.

And that your mom has a nice voice, too.

But your dad sounds like a garbage truck

when he sings!

That's so funny."

I didn't think that was funny *at all*.

"Pearl called my dad a *garbage truck*?" I said.
I forgot all about the nice compliments
about me and my mom.
I focused only on my dad.
My face was *burning*!
Pearl should *never* say mean things about my dad,
even if he doesn't sing well.
He was always very nice to her.
He made up songs about her!
He thought of her as *ours*!
And she wasn't allowed to talk bad
about how I trained my puppy, either.
I got madder and madder,
thinking about what she'd said.

And by the time she came back,

holding a new instruction sheet,

I just wanted her to go away.

The only thing I said to her

during the whole rest of the lab was,

"You put in too much powder.

That's why our bouncy ball won't bounce."

She tried talking to me later,

in and out of class.

The way she always did.

But I shrugged her off

or shook my head.

Until finally she stopped trying.

She just looked at me now and then.

Maybe waiting for me to talk first.

Only,

I didn't.

CHAPTER ELEVEN

Antoine peed
right in the middle of
my parents' bed
the next night.
Even though he was already
very housebroken.

I think he knew
bad things
were about to happen.
I think he knew
doggie camp was going to begin
the very next morning.

"We're never leaving our bedroom door open again,"

my mom told my dad

as they stripped the peed-on sheets off their bed.

"Don't be mad," I said.

"Antoine's *scared*. That's why he did it."

"Maybe he could learn to bite his nails instead,"

my dad said.

"Do you think doggie camp teaches nail-biting?"

"Don't joke about doggie camp," my mom said.

"I'm counting on doggie camp."

She shook her head at Antoine

as she gathered the dirty sheets and bedspread.

Then she and my dad left, to do laundry.

I knelt down beside my dog.

He lay flat on his belly, with his chin on the floor.

His ears looked even floppier than usual.

"Don't be scared," I told him.

"Camp is only two weeks.

Even if you hate it at first,

you'll get used to it.

And the end will go by fast."

For a second I wondered

if Pearl would think I was being too nice to Antoine.

But then I decided,

I didn't care what Pearl thought.

I could be nice to my dog if I wanted to.

CHAPTER TWELVE

The next morning,
my mom asked me
to put together a big bag for Antoine,
with his food
and bones
and favorite toys
and the blanket he loves to sleep on.

I didn't want to gather his things.
Because that would make it easier for him to go.
But I knew what he loved best
and what he'd miss most.
And I wanted to make sure he had everything.
So I put together his bag.

Then I put Antoine on his leash,

and our family went downstairs together.

To wait for the doggie camp van.

It was supposed to arrive at 10:00 that morning.

But we were still waiting at 10:18.

"I hope they haven't forgotten," my mom said.

"*I* hope they *have*," I said.

A squirrel ran by,

and I had to keep Antoine from chasing it.

Then he said hello to Duchess,

the giant poodle

that lives in the apartment below us.

Finally,

a white van pulled up.

It had these words painted on the side:

YIP-YAP U

A COLLEGE FOR CANINES

"We're sending Antoine to *college*?" I said.

"They're just being clever," my mom said.

"He won't go to Harvard until he's eighteen,"
my dad said.

"*Everyone* is being clever," my mom said.

And then a tall man with very curly hair
hopped out of the van.

"You must be the Kanes," he said to us.

"I'm Pete."

After the grown-ups shook hands,
Pete crouched down in front of Antoine.

I wanted Antoine to growl at him.

Maybe even nip.

Instead, he wagged his tail.

Especially when Pete started feeding him treats.

That's cheating, I thought.

I glared at Pete, the big fat cheat,

who'd come to take my dog from me.

But he didn't notice.

He was too busy rubbing

the little space between Antoine's eyes.

"We're going to be good friends, aren't we?"

he said to Antoine.

Then he stood back up

and glanced at his watch.

"Traffic," he said, shaking his head.

"It's already set me back,
and I have two more dogs to pick up."
"Here you go," my dad said,
handing over Antoine's bag.
Pete slung it over his shoulder
and scooped Antoine up with one hand.
"Put him *down!*" I wanted to say.
I hadn't even said good-bye!
Maybe Pete understood,
because he said to Antoine,
"Give everyone some love."
We all gathered around
and said a quick good-bye.
"We'll miss you, little guy,"
my dad said, rubbing Antoine's neck.
"I want you to have fun," my mom told Antoine.
And I said, "Don't be scared."
Then Pete put Antoine's bag
and Antoine

in the van.

"Don't worry," he said.

"I've got him in a doggie seat belt.

Very safe and comfy."

I could see Antoine through the van window,

sitting on the seat,

all buckled up.

Looking confused.

I hated that we were giving him to a stranger.

"What's your last name?" I shouted at Pete

as he walked around the van.

He shouted back something

that sounded like "Pain!"

"We don't know *anything* about that man,"

I told my parents.

"Please don't worry," my mom said.

"Everything will be fine."

Then Pete Pain climbed into the van.

And we all watched

as he drove my dog

farther and farther away.

"I'm having bad memories," I said.

"I'm remembering Bibi,

waving good-bye."

"Me, too," my parents both said, together.

Because when I was eight,

my very special babysitter, Bibi,

rode off, too.

In the backseat of a cab.

And moved to Florida, forever.

"Antoine will be back," my mom said,

"in two short weeks."

"He might have to escape from Pete," I said.

I imagined Pete with a mask on,

carrying Antoine in a sack.

And Antoine struggling to get out.

"He will *not* have to *escape* from Pete,"

my mom said.

"I give you my solemn promise."

"So do I," my dad said.

He put his arm around me,

and I decided to believe both of them

as we all went upstairs together.

CHAPTER THIRTEEN

When we walked into our apartment,

I knew exactly what I wanted to do.

I wanted to hear Bibi's voice.

So I picked up the phone,

and I called her.

I didn't even have to ask my parents for her number.

Because I know Bibi's number

and her mailing address

by heart.

"My Ellie!" she said,

as soon as she heard my voice.

(Ellie is Bibi's nickname for me.

I don't let anyone else use it.)

"How are you?" she asked.

"I'm terrible!" I said.

I told her all about Antoine leaving.

"I wish I could call him, like I'm calling you," I said.

"Or write to him.

But he doesn't talk or read!"

"He'll be home soon," Bibi said.

"Then everything will be fine."

"Definitely not everything," I said.

I told her then

how I'd lost my Mondays and Wednesdays

with Pearl.

And how I had to be a singing rabbit

because of Pearl.

And,

worst of all,

how my feelings had been hurt by Pearl.

"I know my dad doesn't sing well," I told Bibi.

"And maybe I could be better with Antoine.

But why did Pearl have to say that to *Ainsley*?"

Bibi was quiet for a second.

Then she said,

"Sometimes it's hard,

keeping thoughts to ourselves."

I tried then

to remember times when *I'd* had trouble

keeping thoughts to myself.

I couldn't think of a single one!

And I knew I wouldn't have had *any* trouble

keeping my thoughts from Ainsley,

if I'd been Pearl.

I wanted to say,

"It's not hard at all!"

But I didn't want to tell Bibi she was wrong.

So I changed the subject instead.

We talked about her dad

and how he wasn't sick anymore.

And we talked about

how much we missed each other.

Then we hung up.

And it was only days later that I realized:

I'd been wrong,

not Bibi.

Because sometimes

I *did* have trouble—

lots of trouble—

keeping thoughts to myself.

CHAPTER FOURTEEN

When I got to school the next morning,
I sat on a bench in the lobby.
I figured I'd sit there reading
until the warning bell rang.
Because I didn't want to see Pearl.
Only,
before I could even pull out my book,
Pearl walked into the lobby
and saw me.
And
before I could decide whether to hurry away,
she headed straight over
and sat down beside me!
"Hey," she said.
Very quietly, for Pearl.

I didn't answer—

I hadn't figured out what to say.

That's why I'd been trying to *avoid* her.

She looked worried.

Then she said, "Did I do something bad?

Or say something wrong?

I know you're mad at me.

But I can't think of why!"

I hesitated.

Then I said,

"You talked to Ainsley about me.

I don't like that."

Pearl looked confused.

"I must've said good things," she said.

"No, you didn't!" I said.

"You said I'm too nice to Antoine

and my dad sings like a garbage truck.

She told me that!"

"*Oh,*" Pearl said,

covering her mouth with her hand.

Obviously remembering.

"I'm so sorry," she said.

"I wasn't trying to be mean!

I was just telling her about you.

Because you're my best friend!"

"How could 'garbage truck' *not* be mean?" I said.

"And how could it *not* be mean

to say I'm bad with my dog?"

"It came out wrong!" Pearl said.

Her voice was quivery.

Then she said,

"I don't want you to be mad at me!

You're as important to me

as paper is to pencil!"

"You hurt my feelings," I said.

My voice was quivery, too.

We both sat there,

very miserable.

Then Pearl sat up a little straighter.

I could tell she'd had an idea.

So I said, "What?"

And she said,

"How about if I tell *you* something about *Ainsley*?

Would that make things fair?"

"What do you mean?" I said. "What kind of thing?"

Pearl looked to her right

and to her left,

like a spy.

Then she whispered in my ear,

"Ainsley has a crush on Adam."

"She *does*?" I said,

too loudly.

I'd never dreamed of anyone ever

having a crush on Adam.

Pearl nodded, then whispered,

"She thinks he's cute."

"Adam?" I said,

making sure I'd heard right.

Adam was a nice person.

And smart, too.

But *cute?*

"Shhh," Pearl said with wide eyes.

"You have to *promise* never to tell anyone.

It's a secret.

I *swore* I wouldn't tell."

"I promise," I said.

We smiled at each other

for the first time in forever

as the warning bell rang.

Then we hurried together to class.

CHAPTER FIFTEEN

I watched Ainsley later that day, in gym,
as she dribbled the soccer ball
through cones.
And I did a lot of wondering.

I wondered what it would feel like
to have a crush on someone.

I wondered how she knew she had a crush.

I wondered if she wanted to walk down the street
holding Adam's hand.

I wondered how she could *possibly* want that.
I wondered if she liked gum as much as Adam does.

Or if she liked the way his hair sticks up in the back.

I wondered whether he liked her humongous bows.

And then I had to stop wondering.
Because it was my turn to dribble the soccer ball.
And I am very bad at that.
So I had to *focus*.

CHAPTER SIXTEEN

Ainsley did a funny thing

after gym.

She came up to me while I was at my locker.

She had one hand behind her back.

"I want to give you something," she said.

Then,

while I stood there, confused,

she held out

a folded pale pink sweatshirt.

"That's for *me*?" I asked her.

She nodded. She looked a little shy.

"My mom designs sweatshirts," she said.

"I noticed you like stars.

So this one reminded me of you."

I unfolded it.

That sweatshirt was *covered*
with stars of all sizes,
all made out of rhinestones.
"Wow!" I said. "It's so sparkly!"
The truth is,
I would *never* have picked that sweatshirt out
for myself.
But still.
It was very, very nice of her
to think of me.
I felt bad
that I hadn't thought of her at all,

except for my upset thoughts

about her and Pearl.

I tried to think fast.

I had an idea that I knew was stupid,

but I said it anyway.

Because it was all I could come up with.

"Um," I said.

"My mom raises money for hospitals.

Would you like one of her brochures?"

My mom had stacks of those colorful things

in her office.

"No thanks," Ainsley said,

laughing a little.

"I don't want anything, really.

I just thought you'd like the sweatshirt.

My mom's making one for Pearl, too.

But not exactly the same.

It'll be pale pink with sparkly stripes

instead of stars."

I grinned at her.

I couldn't believe how nice she was being.

Still,

a tiny part of me was thinking,

I don't like sweatshirts covered in rhinestones!

And I know Pearl doesn't, either!

CHAPTER SEVENTEEN

We had our first rehearsal that afternoon.
Mrs. Quaid asked us to sit in a circle
with our scripts
on the stage in the auditorium.
I sat on the smooth wooden floor next to Katie
and tried not to look out
on the rows and rows of audience seats.

I tried not to think about parents and kids

filling those seats

and watching me.

I focused on Mrs. Quaid instead.

She was sitting across the circle,

between Nicholas and Adam.

"I brought us a snack," Mrs. Quaid said.

"Carrot sticks and carrot juice.

Rabbity favorites!"

I don't like carrot sticks,

and I would *never* drink carrot juice—

it smells *disgusting*!

So I just waited,

and wished that rabbits loved brookies,

while other kids ate and drank.

When they'd finally finished, Mrs. Quaid said,

"For this first rehearsal,

we'll read through the script.
Pay no attention to the songs, for now.
Just read your lines
loudly and *clearly*."
She put on her glasses and opened her script.
Then she looked at me and asked,
"Ready to start us off?"
I nodded
and cleared my throat
and started to read.

In the first scene,
I, Mama Rabbit, get arrested
and thrown in the bunny dungeon
because the Hop Cops think—
wrongly!—
that I've robbed a Hare Salon.

I read the lines in that scene *loudly* and *clearly*.

Because they're not embarrassing at all.
Nicholas gave me a big thumbs-up
at the end of the scene.
Which was nice of him.

But after that,
I got quieter and quieter,
and I mumbled more and more.
Because my other lines
were *ridiculous*.

I call Nicholas
(my bunny son)
"Honey Bunny"
and "Sweet Honey Bun"
and "Oh, Angel Mine."

I say things like,
"Without me to care for you,

Honey Bunny,
how will you *survive*?"

And
"Your sweet honey bun fur
is as soft as marshmallow Peeps."

I couldn't look at Nicholas after those lines.
Or anywhere near him.
But I was pretty certain
he didn't give *them* a thumbs-up.

Other kids giggled.
Someone made smooching sounds.

And all I wanted
was to crawl behind the curtains
at the back of the stage.

Then
Katie said,
"Eleanor? Are you blushing?"
And freckly Ben said,
"Yes! She's practically *purple*!"
And Nicholas said,
"Leave her alone."

That should've been a good thing.
Nicholas was being so nice.
But
for some reason,
it made me blush *more*.
Which made me feel *worse*.

And then

came the most embarrassing moment of all.

The moment when the script says

I have to hug Nicholas.

Ben sang out,

"Eleanor and Nicholas,

sitting in a tree,

K-I-S-S-I-N-G."

Mrs. Quaid made him stop

before he could start the "first comes love" part.

"I expect more from you," she said

to all the laughing kids.

But everyone kept laughing.

I wanted to crawl behind the curtains *and*

pull them down on top of me.

I guess I'm not *mature,* I thought.
And then I thought,
I can't stand another second of this.

Luckily, I didn't have to.
With that hug, we'd finished the script.

"See you Wednesday!" Mrs. Quaid said.
I leapt off the stage then
and ran up an aisle of the auditorium
and out the door.

CHAPTER EIGHTEEN

All through breakfast
and my whole walk to school the next morning,
I hoped, hoped, hoped
that everyone had forgotten
the K-I-S-S-I-N-G.
But of course they hadn't.
As soon as I walked into my classroom,
not long before the first bell,
Katie and Ben ran over to me.
"You were so *embarrassed* yesterday," Katie said.
"It was *hilarious*!" Ben said.
Which was so mean!
He was laughing at me!
I didn't think things could possibly get worse.
But then Katie,

who is supposed to be my *friend*, said,
"*Why* did you get so embarrassed?
It's just a play."
She thought for a second and said,
"Unless you *do* have a crush on Nicholas,
in real life."
"I *don't!*" I said.
"You do keep all his pictures in your desk,"
Katie said. "You've shown me."
"I keep them because they're *good!*" I said.
"That doesn't *mean* anything!"
"Maybe it means you have a crush on him,
deep down," Katie said.
"I do *not*
have a deep-down *crush*
on Nicholas!" I practically shouted.
I wanted to cry.
If Katie didn't believe me,
maybe no one would!

And why did she have to say that in front of *Ben*?
Right away, he started chanting,
"Eleanor has a crush on Nich-o-las!
Eleanor has a crush on Nich-o-las!"
In that horrible moment,
Ainsley and Pearl walked through the door.

I saw Ainsley
and I heard "crush"
and I put the two together.
I wanted to stop Ben's chanting.
I *needed* to stop Ben's chanting!
Because *everyone* was listening
and *everyone* was staring—
and so I did something very stupid
and very mean.
I said, "*I* don't have a crush on Nicholas,
but *Ainsley* has a crush on *Adam*!"

Everyone turned and stared at Ainsley.

"You have a crush on Adam?" Katie said.

Ainsley's face flushed pink

and her mouth dropped open.

Then she said, "*What?*"

"Eleanor said you have a crush on Adam," Ben said.

I wanted to cry out, "No, I didn't!"

But everyone had heard me!

"How did Eleanor—" Ainsley said.

"I never—" Ainsley said.

Then she narrowed her eyes

and turned and *glared* at Pearl

and said, "You *told* her? That was a *secret!*"
"I'm so sorry!" Pearl said.
Then Pearl turned to *me*
and gave me a look she'd never, ever
given me before.
That look said,
How could *you?*
and
I was wrong to ever trust you.

My heart ripped in pieces.

"I didn't mean—" I started to say.
"I was just joking!" I tried to tell everyone.
But nobody listened.
Because Adam and Nicholas were
walking into the room.
"What happened?" Adam asked,

when everyone stared at him.
And that's when Ainsley started crying
and ran from the room.

Pearl ran after her.

And I covered my face with my hands.
I *hated* that I hadn't kept that secret.
My whole body felt sweaty.
And I kept thinking,
over and over,
I am going to throw up.
I really am.

CHAPTER NINETEEN

I froze there
for two seconds.

Then I ran out of the room, too.

I had to follow Pearl and Ainsley.
I *had* to apologize.

I figured they'd probably be in the bathroom.
So I ran there first.
A kindergartner was standing on a step stool,
washing her hands.
I rushed past her
and checked all of the stalls.
They were empty,

except the one farthest from the door.
I looked under the door of that stall
and saw two pairs of feet:
Pearl's sneakers
and Ainsley's glittery flats.
I felt a tiny bit of relief,
seeing those four feet together.

Maybe Ainsley won't hate Pearl forever
because of me, I thought.
Then I banged on the door.
"It's Eleanor!" I said loudly,
so they'd be sure to hear me.
"I'm *so* sorry!
I am *so, so* sorry!"
I heard a sniffle.
Then I heard someone whisper something.
It sounded like "oh away."
Then Pearl called through the door,
"Ainsley wants you to go away.
I want you to go away."
I felt like I'd been punched in the face.
Then *I* started crying.
My best friend,
Pearl,
wanted me to go away.
And it was all my fault.

"I didn't mean to do it!" I said
in a high and shaky voice.
I squeezed my eyes shut
and tried to *think*
about how I could fix this.
"I'll keep taking it back," I said.
"I'll tell everyone I didn't mean it.
I'll put up posters
saying Ainsley barely even *knows* Adam."
That made Ainsley cry *louder*.
"I want to move back to Orlando!" she wailed.
"Eleanor, you *have* to go away!" Pearl yelled.
And so I turned to run away.
I saw then
that the kindergartner was still on her stool,
with water still gushing out of the faucet.
She was staring at me with huge eyes
through the mirror.
"You're wasting water!" I told her,

in a voice that was much too mean.
Which was *another* bad thing I did!
Because I was upset!
She turned off the water, quick,
and I finally ran from there.
I didn't even bother going back to class.
I went straight to the school nurse instead.
I needed her to send me *home*.

CHAPTER TWENTY

I did not have to lie to the nurse.

Because I was actually feeling terrible.

"My stomach hurts," I told her. "My head, too.
And I just want to go to sleep."

"Which side of your stomach hurts?" she asked.

"The whole thing," I said.

She took my temperature then
and called my mom.
"Eleanor doesn't have a fever," she said.
"But she doesn't feel good. Or look good, either.
I think she's coming down with something."
Then the nurse listened for a second
and said, "I'll let her know."
She hung up the phone and told me,
"Your mom will be here very soon.
Why don't you go to your cubby
and gather what you need."
I felt a little lighter then.
I was going home!
The hallway was empty
because everyone else was in class.
I felt relieved, not seeing anybody.
But that didn't last long.
Because
after I got to my cubby

and started gathering everything I thought I'd need,
I noticed some pale pink fabric
wadded up
in a back corner.

My heart fell then.

I knew exactly what that fabric was.
It was the sparkly sweatshirt Ainsley had given me,
so very nicely.
The one her mom had made.

I lifted it slowly out of my cubby
and unwadded it.
It had been so neat and smooth and new
when Ainsley gave it to me.
Now it was wrinkled
and covered with greasy cookie crumbs
and marked up

all over
with ink.

I tried to brush off the crumbs,
but the chocolate left streaks.
And my eyes filled with tears.
I should've taken care of that sweatshirt!
I should've brought it home
and kept it safe in a dresser drawer
and *worn* it today
and said to everyone,
"Ainsley's mom made this sweatshirt!
Isn't it *great*?"
Instead of saying she had a crush on Adam!
She'd given me a present, just to be nice.
And I'd ruined that present
and her life!

I stopped brushing crumbs off the sweatshirt

and licked my finger
and tried to get out the chocolate.
And the ink.
That's how my mom found me:
scrubbing at my pale pink sweatshirt
with a finger covered in spit.
"There you are," she said. "How are you feeling?"
I shook the sweatshirt at her.
"You have to get the stains out!" I said.
"You *have* to!"
She looked at me funny.
"I mean it!" I cried.
She put her arm around me
and said, "Let's get you home.
You can explain on the way."
So I explained, slowly, on the way.
A lot of it was hard to say.
I didn't know how she'd react
when I got to the part

about announcing Ainsley's secret.
I thought she'd get mad at me
or say, "*Eleanor,*"
in a very disappointed tone.
But she didn't say anything at all.
She just looked very sad
and very serious.
When I'd finished my whole story, she said,
"There's a lot to fix, isn't there?"
I nodded. There *was* a lot to fix.
"We might as well start with the sweatshirt,"
my mom said.
"But your dad is the stain magician, not me."
"Right," I said.
I'd forgotten—that was true.
And then my mom said,
"We'll see what he can do."

CHAPTER TWENTY-ONE

Being home
wasn't great.
My mom had to get right on a work call.
"I'm sorry about this," she said.
"But it's important.
And it's been planned forever."
I wished, wished, wished
I could play with Antoine
while Mom was shut inside her office.
Or curl up on the couch
with Antoine beside me.
But he was gone.

I curled up on the couch anyway,

without him,

for a little while.

But just lying on the couch,

thinking,

I kept seeing Pearl's face in my head—

that moment when she realized

she should never have trusted me.

And I kept remembering Ainsley wailing,

"I want to move back to Orlando!"

I had to jump off the couch

and stop thinking.

But then I didn't know *what* to do.

I could watch TV, I thought.

That's what I usually did,

as a special treat,

when I was sick.

But I knew I couldn't *actually* watch TV.

Because I wasn't actually sick.
And I definitely didn't deserve
a special treat.

I stood for a second near the couch,
just looking at the turned-off TV.
It's impossible at school, I thought,
and it's impossible here.
I'll never be happy again.

That's when I heard our front door open.
My dad called out,
"I'm home!"
Even though it was very early
for him to leave work.
I ran to him,
and he gave me a hug.
"Your mom called me
right when you got home," he said,

while I was still wrapped in the hug.

"I gather things aren't going well."

I nodded,

my face pressed against his shirt.

"Right," he said,

letting me go.

"Let's talk.

But first I must gather

my stain-fighting supplies."

I ran and got Ainsley's sweatshirt.

I'd folded it neatly

and put it on top of my dresser.

Then I met my dad in the kitchen.

He was setting sponges

and cornstarch

and seltzer

and spot-removing sticks

on the counter.

"Different stains require different techniques," he said.

Then he reached for the sweatshirt.

"Hmm," he said,

examining the different stains.

I held my breath,

thinking he might say it was ruined forever.

Instead he said,

"I'm up to the challenge."

Then he went to work on one of the stains

with cornstarch and a sponge.

"Did I ever tell you," he said,

as he scrubbed at the stain,

"about the worst thing I ever did to your mom?"

"No," I said,

very shocked.

"*You* did something bad to *Mom*?"

He nodded

and added cornstarch to the sweatshirt.

"It was before we were married," he said.

"She called me one night

when we were seniors in college.
Her alarm clock had broken.
She had a job interview the next morning.
She asked me to set *my* alarm
and call her in the morning, to wake her up.
So she wouldn't miss her interview."
He glanced at me,
then said,
"She really wanted that job."
He started rubbing very hard on a stain
with the spot-removing stick.
"What happened?" I asked.
Now he gave me a very guilty look.
"I forgot," he said.
"I didn't set my alarm.
She slept through the interview
and didn't get the job."
He looked so sad,
I thought he might actually cry.

And this had happened *forever* ago!

"She trusted me," he said.

"She needed me.

And I blew it."

I felt very bad for him then.

Even though I knew

she'd married him in the end.

"What'd you *do*?" I asked.

He poured a little seltzer on the sweatshirt.

"She was *mad*," he said.

"Understandably!

I apologized *many* times.

I bought her flowers.

I offered to call the interview people

and explain.

Nothing worked.

Until"—

he looked at me and grinned—

"I stood outside her dorm window one night,

with a boom box raised above my head."

"What's a boom box?" I said.

"A portable stereo," he said.

"It was old-fashioned even then.

But it was like a scene

from a movie we loved.

I played one of her favorite songs

on that boom box,

very loudly.

And I sang along."

"With your voice?" I said.

Because even though I hated when Pearl said it,

he *did* sound like a garbage truck when he sang.

"With my voice," he said.

"I attracted quite a crowd.

She had to forgive me

and let me in.

Just to shut me up.

And the rest,

as they say,

is history."

He shook out Ainsley's sweatshirt then.

"We all make mistakes," he said.

"The important thing

is to keep trying to make up for them,

for as long as it takes."

He held the sweatshirt up for me to see.

It looked pasty

and splotchy.

"My stain-fighting magic needs time to set," he said.

"And then we need to wash the whole sweatshirt

in hot water.

Do you want to wear it tomorrow?"

I nodded.

"And every single day for the rest of the year," I said.

"If I have to."

He nodded

and said, "I like the way you're thinking."

CHAPTER
TWENTY—TWO

The next morning, before the bell,
I was too scared to walk into my classroom.
I didn't want to see *anyone*
who knew what had happened
the day before.

I wanted so badly
to hide in the bathroom.
But I couldn't!
Because what if Pearl and Ainsley were
back in their stall?
Or
what if the kindergartner was there?

The poor, cute kindergartner
that I'd *yelled* at?

Instead of the bathroom,
I stuck my head in my cubby
for a very long time,
pretending to look for something.
I heard crowds of kids walk by.
I ignored them all.
I ignored the pain in my neck
and back and shoulders, too.
Until the warning bell rang.
And I had no choice.
I had to go in.

As soon as I stepped into the classroom,
I noticed Adam and Ben
at the back of the room,
tossing a squishy football
and laughing.

135

Like *nothing* had happened!
I glared at those happy boys.
Especially Ben,
who'd started *everything* with his stupid chanting!

And then Mrs. Ramji exclaimed, "Eleanor!"
I turned to her quickly
and held my breath.
Was she mad at me?
Had she heard about my meanness?
She didn't look mad.
"I love your sweatshirt!" she said. "It's so *lively*!"
"Thanks," I said.

I glanced over at Ainsley then.
She was sitting at her desk.
I'd hoped she might smile
if I wore the sweatshirt.
But she was definitely not smiling.

"Ainsley's mom designed it,"
I told Mrs. Ramji quickly.
So Ainsley would hear me give her mom credit.
But Ainsley just frowned deeper.
She looked like
she wanted me
to *take* the sweatshirt *off*.

I crossed my arms over my chest.
I didn't have anything to change into!

"Your mom is very talented, Ainsley,"
Mrs. Ramji said.
Ainsley did smile a little then,
but only at Mrs. Ramji.
And she thanked her.
Then Mrs. Ramji said to the whole class,
"All right, everyone. Let's get started."
So I had to go sit in my seat.

Right next to Pearl.
She wouldn't even look at me.
She leaned *away* from me
and took a notebook out of her backpack.
I'd helped her decorate the outside of that notebook!
But she definitely wasn't having
happy decorating memories.
She set the notebook down, hard, on her desk
and slammed a pen on top of it

and stared straight ahead.

I kept looking at her.
But she wouldn't look back.

"I'm sorry!" I wanted to tell her.
"I'm sorry, I'm sorry, I'm sorry, I'm sorry.
I'm *so* sorry."
But I'd already tried that.
And she'd told me to *go away*.

My shoulders slumped a little,
and I shook my head.
I'd never get Pearl back.
We'd never be friends again.
She'd never tell me one of her poems
or call me on the phone and shout,
"Eleanor! It's Pearl!"

I was starting to cry
in school
for the second day in a row,
when a wadded-up ball of paper flew through the air
and landed on my desk.

I knew exactly what that flying piece of paper was.

I opened it up
and smoothed it out.
Sure enough, Nicholas Rigby had drawn me a picture.

This one had a little row of chicks.
He'd labeled them "Marshmallow Peeps."
And he'd written,
right above them,
"Don't be sad."

I wiped tears off my cheeks
and folded that picture neatly
and put it on top of the pile of pictures
I kept in my desk.
Then I turned and whispered to him, "Thanks,"
like I always did.
He kicked the back of my chair,
not too hard,
like he always did.

And I had to admit,
he'd made me feel better.

CHAPTER TWENTY-THREE

Nicholas's note gave me an idea.
Maybe a note could help
with Ainsley
and with Pearl.
So,
while Mrs. Ramji talked about multiplying by ten,
I thought hard about what I wanted to say
to each of them.
Then,
as quietly as I could,
I tore two pieces of paper
out of my notebook.
And I wrote to them both.

First, I wrote this note to Ainsley:

Dear Ainsley,

I am so sorry.

I hope you will forgive me someday.

I'm planning to wear this sweatshirt

every single day

until you do.

Except

I don't think you will like that.

Will you PLEASE tell me

if you don't want me to?

And if there's something else I can do?

PLEASE tell me.

Your friend,

who shouldn't have done what she did,

Eleanor

And then I wrote to Pearl.

I'd decided she might like a poem.

Since she talks like a poet sometimes.

So I wrote:

> Dear Pearl,
>
> I did a mean thing.
>
> A very mean thing.
>
> To a new girl AND
>
> to my best friend.
>
> I HATE that I did it.
>
> But I did.
>
> This is worse than
>
> carrot juice on a cupcake
>
> or a wasp on my pillow
>
> or a dress that's too tight at the neck.
>
> I hope you never do anything that mean.
>
> I really do.

I almost ended my note there,
with the end of that poem.
But then I worried
that it wasn't enough.
So I kept going.
I added:

I am so sorry.
I will do ANYTHING to make it up to you.
I would eat PICKLES for you.

You are still my very best friend,
even if I am not yours.

I am so, so, so sorry.

Love,
Eleanor

As soon as I finished writing to Pearl and Ainsley,

I pretended I needed a tissue.

I walked over to the tissue box by the window.

As I passed Pearl,

I slipped her note on her desk.

And I did the same for Ainsley.

Then I pretended to blow my nose by the window.

I tried to watch Pearl and Ainsley while I did.

Ainsley didn't even open my note.

She just put it in her backpack.

Pearl did read hers.

I think she even smiled a tiny bit.

And then she wrote me back!

I was so happy

when I saw her put that note on my desk,

I almost ran back there.

And I opened that note up fast.

But

it only said:

You would never eat pickles.

CHAPTER TWENTY-FOUR

I knew what I had to do
as soon as I read Pearl's note.
I waited
and waited
and waited
for lunch,
tapping my fingers on my desk
until Mrs. Ramji asked me to stop.
"Your new sweatshirt is giving you energy!"
she said. "But the noise is distracting."
I sat on my hands after that,
until it was finally time for lunch.
Then I stood in the cafeteria line

with my plastic tray.

And as soon as I got to the front,

I said to the lunch lady,

"Can I *please* have a pickle?"

"We're not serving pickles today," she said.

"It's cold cuts day tomorrow.

You'll have to wait until then."

"I can't!" I said.

I got ready to climb over the steaming meatballs

and push past that lady

and search the kitchen myself.

"It's an *emergency*!" I told the lunch lady.

She squinted at me.

I put my hand on my heart,

to show how much I meant it.

"So," she said,

"this is a life-or-death pickle?"

"It is!" I said. "I *swear*."

"We only have pickle slices," she said.

"That's fine!" I said.

She shook her head

and wiped her hands on her apron.

"How many?" she asked.

It was a good question!

Just one slice might not impress Pearl.

But I couldn't eat too many!

I'd vomit all over the cafeteria!

The poor lunch lady might have to help clean it up!

"Two, please," I told her.

She left then, to get the pickles.

Kids behind me in line

started getting restless.

I ignored them.

My problems were bigger than theirs.

Finally the lunch lady came back, holding

a small white bowl

with two pickle slices.
I thanked her a million times
and hurried away,
without any actual lunch.
I searched the cafeteria,
holding my little bowl,
until I saw Ainsley and Pearl.
There were no empty seats at their table,
but I didn't need one.
I walked over to Pearl
and set the bowl on the table, next to her plate.
She looked up at me,
very surprised.
I lifted one slimy, dripping wet pickle slice
with my fingers.
I could barely look at it!
And it stank so badly!
But still.
I held my nose

and took a sour, nasty bite

and swallowed.

I didn't even have a drink!

I didn't think I could take too many more

of those bites.

But I had to finish two whole slices!

I closed my eyes.

I could feel Pearl watching me.

"What is she *doing*?" someone at the table said.

"Shh!" Pearl told them.

The whole table went silent.

I made a big decision.

I was still holding the rest of the slice.

I grabbed the other slice, too,

and shoved them both in my mouth at once;

and,

with my eyes squeezed shut,

I chewed and chewed

as fast as I could

and
swallowed.
"Wow," I heard Pearl say.
Then,
without my even asking,
she handed me her water.

CHAPTER
TWENTY-FIVE

I'd hoped Pearl and I could play together
during recess that afternoon.
Because she'd given me water!
And after lunch, she'd started smiling at me again!
But *Ainsley*
was still not smiling.
And Pearl chose Ainsley
over me.
Together,
the whole entire recess,
they did a fancy hand-clapping game
that I'd never seen before!
Ainsley must've taught it to Pearl

one Monday or Wednesday afternoon
when *Pearl* was supposed to be teaching *Ainsley*.

I sat by myself on a bench
while they clapped and sang.
And I tried to *think*.
Because I needed another plan.

Finally,
as the recess bell rang,
I had an idea.

I needed to talk to Pearl and Ainsley right away.
I hurried behind them
and saw them walk into the bathroom.
I decided to follow them in.
Even though I did *not*
have good memories
of that place.

At least there was no one else in the bathroom
this time.
And Pearl and Ainsley weren't sharing a stall,
with Ainsley weeping inside.
I could see Pearl's sneakers in the stall by the wall
and Ainsley's flats in the next stall down.

"Um," I said.
To get their attention.
Then I said, "It's Eleanor. I've been thinking—
what if we promise that you will never
tell *me* someone else's secret,
and I will never tell *you* someone else's secret?
If someone shares a secret with you,
I don't want to know about it!
Ever!
Then could we be friends?
Because I *hate*
not being friends!"

For a second,
neither of them spoke.

Then Pearl cried out from behind her door,
"I don't want to be told secrets, either!
And I *definitely* won't tell.
I wish I could erase sharing Ainsley's secret.
I should *never* have done that!"

Pearl and I both waited then,
for Ainsley to say something.

Finally,
in a little voice,
Ainsley said,
"Do we have to do this
while I'm peeing?
Could I talk to Pearl about it later?"

"Yes, definitely!" Pearl said. "We'll talk later!"
And I said, "Okay."

But I thought,
Why can't I talk about it, too?
It's my idea!

I left them in the bathroom then.
For the second day in a row.
But at least
this time,
I wasn't running
to the nurse.

CHAPTER TWENTY-SIX

Mrs. Quaid let us practice in our bunny costumes
at rehearsal that afternoon.

"We won't do this often," she said.

"But it helps give you a feel for your characters."

Those soft, furry costumes
zipped right over our clothes.
And we each got a headband
with two giant ears attached!
My costume was lavender,
and Katie's was yellow,
and Nicholas's was pale blue.
We all had white bellies and paws and ears.

I liked seeing my friends as bunnies
and being one myself.
But still.
I dreaded the solo
and hugging Nicholas.

I got ready to *punch* freckly Ben
with my rabbit paw
if he started chanting *anything*.
I'd never punched anyone in my life.
But I'd never eaten pickles, either,
before that day.
I figured I'd punch Ben twice.
Once for me
and once for Ainsley.

When everyone was in costume,
Mrs. Quaid said, "Let's begin with scene two."
I closed my eyes for a second

and shook my head,
knowing what was coming.
And sure enough,
as soon as I said my first "Honey Bun,"
Ben said, *"Oooh."*

I stopped reading my lines then
and put my paws on my hips
and *glared* at him.
"That's *enough*, Ben,"
Mrs. Quaid said,
very sharply.
And Katie said, "Definitely."
And Nicholas said, "Yeah—*definitely.*"
Which was very nice of them.
Ben shrugged
and started pulling on one of Adam's ears.
"Be careful, Ben!" Mrs. Quaid said.
"Those ears rip!"

Adam put his hand on his bunny ear then
and said,
"It's bleeding! It's *bleeding*!"
Everyone laughed.

And
from that moment on,
nobody paid any attention
to my lines.
It was so much easier, too,
to remember that it was just a play
when I was dressed as a rabbit.
So I read my lines loudly and clearly
and felt braver and braver.

Even the hugging scene went well,
because Nicholas and I just waved at each other
instead of hugging.
Mrs. Quaid shook her head and said,

"We'll let that be enough for today."
Then we kept going.

Best of all,
once again,
I didn't have to sing my solo.
"We'll focus on your song next time,"
Mrs. Quaid told me.
"But here's your job, from now until the show.
You must practice convincing yourself
that you are *not* Eleanor.
You are a famous singer
who performs in front of crowds.
Do you have a favorite singer?"
"Not really," I said.
"Give it some thought," she said.
"My dad likes the Beatles," I said.
"They're famous, right? I could be one of them."
"That would be perfect," she said.

We took off our bunny costumes then.

And I realized

that my sweatshirt had gotten a little sweaty.

It was hot under all that fur!

I have to ask Mom to wash it, I thought.

Because I was still determined

to wear that sweatshirt every single day

until Ainsley forgave me.

CHAPTER
TWENTY—SEVEN

I worried the next morning as I walked to school,
wearing my clean sweatshirt.
What if Ainsley didn't like my no-secrets plan?
What if she stayed mad?
Would Pearl be friends with me anyway?
Would she ever play with *me* at recess?
And be partners with *me* in science?
Or would she always choose Ainsley?

My dad told me everything would be okay
as he kissed me good-bye.

I didn't believe him.

But then I walked into the classroom
and saw Ainsley and Pearl.
They were both wearing pale pink sweatshirts.
Ainsley's was covered in sparkly rhinestone bows.
And Pearl's had sparkly rhinestone stripes.
They waved at me
and I hurried to them,
wearing my own rhinestoned sweatshirt.
We stood together,
smiling at one another—
a very glittery trio.
And then Pearl said,
"I am as happy
as a puppy gulping down
a whole bag of treats."
And I thought,
That's my best friend, Pearl.
She's going to be a famous poet someday.
I just know it.

CHAPTER
TWENTY—EIGHT

The next week flew by.
Rehearsals lasted longer and longer,
and Ainsley and Pearl both started teasing me.
Because I kept humming bunny tunes during class,
and pretending to be one of the Beatles,
and muttering my lines.

But then,
Friday came.
The day of the show.

The only thing I muttered that day was,
"I feel sick."

I wasn't going to be able to do my solo.
I knew I wasn't!
I couldn't pretend to be a Beatle!
They were *men*! And they were *ancient*!
Some of them were even *dead*!
That idea had been ridiculous.

I felt even sicker and shakier after school,
as the cast got ready for the show.
Nicholas burped a few lines of my solo for me.
I knew he was trying to make me laugh,
so I'd be less scared.
But still. It was disgusting.
So it made me feel worse.
And I couldn't eat one of the delicious
golden vanilla cupcakes
decorated with bunny faces
that Mrs. Quaid gave us, as a pre-show treat.
Maybe if they'd been brookie cupcakes—

which I'd never gotten to try—

I could've overcome my feelings of sickness.

But they weren't.

So I wrapped my bunny cupcake in napkins

and set it on a table backstage, for later.

I did *not* save

the carrot juice

that Mrs. Quaid also handed out.

"What drink could be better for rabbits?"

she kept saying.

And I thought,

Who would want carrot juice

anywhere near

a yummy cupcake?

What if it spills?

That would be a tragedy!

After snack time, I zipped into my bunny suit.

Which made me sweaty *and* shaky.

And then Mrs. Quaid said, "Everyone, backstage!"
So,
wearing our furry costumes,
we all crammed into the little space
behind the curtains at the back of the stage.
It was crowded and loud back there.
Mrs. Quaid kept shouting things like,
"Check the props table!
Make sure you have what you need!"
Finally she checked her watch and shouted,
"Quiet down! It's *time*!"

We all rushed to peek through the curtains.
Kids and parents were filling up every seat
in every row!

Suddenly, I *had* to pee.
But there was no time!
Mrs. Quaid was calling,

"Places, everyone! Places!"

And then she said,

"Where's Eleanor?"

I raised my hand and said, "Here."

"The audience lights will go down in a second,"

she told me.

"And then you'll step onstage.

Don't forget your carrot!

Do you have your carrot?"

I *didn't* have my carrot!

I had to shove my way to the props table then,

saying, "Excuse me!

Carrot emergency!"

as I pushed other bunnies aside.

Then I shoved my way back to Mrs. Quaid.

And before I could tell her anything about peeing,

she said,

"Remember: *loudly* and *clearly*!"

She opened the curtain for me.

And I had to step onto the stage.

I heard Mrs. Quaid say, "Shhhh!" behind me.

And then I was standing in silence.

I blinked a few times.

It was hard to see

with the stage lights bright in my eyes

and the houselights off.

But then, right in the middle of the third row,

I saw Pearl and Ainsley grinning up at me.

And my parents, grinning, too.

Pearl started waving and waving,

and I almost waved back!

Then someone coughed, and I realized

I had to *act*.

I stood a little straighter and said,

not very loudly or clearly,

"It was the best of carrots,

it was the worst of carrots."

My voice was shaking.

But still,

I heard grown-ups laugh.

Then Nicholas came onstage.

I think he gave me a thumbs-up,

but it was hard to tell,

because his hands were covered with furry paws.

I spoke louder and clearer after that.

And

for some reason,

my early scenes with Nicholas

were especially easy.

But whenever I was offstage, I kept thinking,

Solo, solo, solo, solo.

My heart was beating to that sound!

Finally,

when that solo was thirty seconds away,

I pushed my way to Mrs. Quaid

and I said,

"Can Nicholas sing with me?

Like at our audition?

I can't do it by myself!"

She put her hands on my shoulders

and looked in my eyes

and said,

"You *can* do it.

You've worked so hard.

Just remember—do *not* be Eleanor!

Now, go!"

And she practically pushed me onto the stage.

The piano started.
I thought,
I can't breathe!
And then I thought,
I'm going to sound like a garbage truck!
I missed my cue from the piano—
I was supposed to be singing.
But instead I was thinking,
Garbage truck!
Then I knew what to do!
The piano started the song again.
I imagined holding a boom box high in the air,
and when I heard my cue the second time around,
I sang my solo right to my mom.
I just pretended I was my dad
outside her window.

As soon as I finished,
Pearl leapt to her feet

and shouted, "Yay, Eleanor!"
Ainsley jumped up, too, clapping and clapping,
and so did both my parents.
I bowed a tiny bit to them.
And then I hurried as fast as I could,
in my furry suit,
off the stage.

The next time I went on,
I had to hug Nicholas.
I'm a rabbit, I'm a rabbit, I'm a rabbit,
I told myself.
And then I hugged him as fast as I could
and stepped back.
Mrs. Quaid shouted out from backstage,
"The end!"
And the whole audience cheered and cheered.
Every bunny in the play came onstage.
Nicholas stood on one side of me

and Katie stood on the other.

We took one another's paws,

and we all bowed together.

Then I heard someone yell, "Eleanor!"

I looked out at my row of fans,

and my dad started tossing flowers on the stage.

That was almost as embarrassing

as hugging Nicholas!

Still,

even with those flowers at my feet,

I was glad I hadn't quit that play.

CHAPTER
TWENTY—NINE

My parents let me eat my bunny-decorated cupcake
(with no disgusting carrot juice anywhere near it)
for breakfast the next morning
as a special treat.
"To celebrate your newfound stardom," my dad said.
That cupcake was very delicious,
even though it wasn't a brookie.
And that wasn't even the best part of my day!
The best part came later,
when Pete Pain brought my dog home.
He parked the Yip-Yap U van
in front of our apartment,
and I ran to unbuckle Antoine.

I hugged that puppy tight.
Then I checked him all over,
for cuts and bruises.
And other signs of torture.
But he looked very healthy.
And he kept licking my face!
"I'm happy to see you, too," I told him.

Pete Pain stayed with us for hours,
teaching us to shout "Ow!"
and stop playing, if Antoine nipped.
And to say "Sit!" instead of "No!" when he jumped.
And to yell "Leave it!" whenever he started to chew.
Pete told us over and over
to always use the exact same commands,
all three of us,
all the time.

I had to admit,

Antoine behaved *very* nicely

during that training session.

Still,

after Pete Pain left, for the whole rest of the day,

I kept Antoine away from my parents' room

and all of their stuff.

I decided to do that

for the whole rest of my life, too.

Because I did *not* want my dog

sent away from me

ever again.

CHAPTER THIRTY

The next Monday in school,
just before the morning bell,
a wadded-up piece of paper flew through the air
and landed on my desk.

I knew exactly what that flying paper was.

I opened it up
and smoothed it out.
Sure enough, Nicholas had drawn me a picture.
But
it was a new kind of picture.

For the first time ever,
Nicholas had drawn himself

with me.
Just the two of us,
together on a stage,
in our bunny suits,
holding each other's paws.

I stared at that picture for a long time.
My heart felt jumpy
and my face felt blush-y
as I looked at just the two of us,
together,
holding each other's paws.

I couldn't stop myself from thinking,
I might like that.

And suddenly, I felt very shy.
I could *not* turn
and look at Nicholas.

So this time, I thanked him
without turning.
He kicked the back of my chair,
not too hard,
like he always did.
Then I folded the picture neatly
and put it on top of the pile in my desk.
Like I always did.

But I already knew
that later,
I'd take that picture out
and put it in my backpack,
so I could carry it home with me
and do some more thinking
about Nicholas,
who'd drawn marshmallow Peeps for me
when I was sad.
And burped my solo for me

when I was scared.
And stood up for me,
twice,
when Ben was mean.

I knew, too,
that I'd sneak that picture into my backpack
when no one was looking.
Not even my best friend, Pearl.
Because
I wanted to keep that picture
and my thoughts about Nicholas
to myself.

At least for a while,
I wanted to keep a secret of my own.